WANTED

The Chocolate Monster

For Rosalie, Laura
and Juniper
P. J.
For Jon and Vicky
L. H.

First published in the UK in 2017
by Faber and Faber Limited
Bloomsbury House,
74–77 Great Russell Street, London WC1B 3DA

Text copyright © Pip Jones, 2017
Illustration copyright © Laura Hughes, 2017

ISBN 978–0–571–32751–5

➤ A FABER PICTURE BOOK ◄

WANTED

The Chocolate Monster

The CHUNK

Written by
Pip Jones

Illustrated by
Laura Hughes

ff

FABER & FABER

Attention kids! Now, listen up –
OFFICIAL PUBLIC WARNING:
A mighty tricky, sticky thief
was spotted just this morning.
One hundred thousand chocolate bars
are offered as reward,
to anyone who helps retrieve
this chocolate monster's hoard.

The Chunk: he's silent, like a cloud.
He walks on tippy-toes.
His hands and feet are HUGE!
He has a bulbous,
twitching nose.

His purple fur is
streaked with pink,
it hides his
gleaming eyes,

And though he's eight
feet high, The Chunk's
a master of disguise.

The Chunk prowls round the neighbourhoods,
sniffing out his booty.

Chocolate's what he's after,
so we need you all on duty.

Keep watch, and close
all cupboard doors.
No chocolate bar's secure.

If left at large, The Chunk will soon
swing by YOUR house, for sure.

He'll tiptoe in,
and start to search
for treats that
might be had.

He'll take the last chocs
from the box . . . and then
he'll blame your dad.

A lovely chocolate pudding,
saved especially for your gran?
Forget it, pal! The Chunk can sniff
out ANY chocolate flan.

Chocolate mousse? Eclairs and cakes?
He'll chomp them just like that,
and then make sure your parents
blame the whole
thing on the cat.

He'll find expensive truffles
and he'll snaffle all that swag,
then stash the wrappers, clear to see,
in your poor mummy's bag.

The Chunk will stop at nothing,
and what he wants he'll take.

He just won't care! Not *even* if he
nicks your birthday cake.

The Chunk will pinch from ANYONE!
Chocolate trifles, chocolate swirls . . .
But kids beware! He's REALLY
got it in for boys and girls!

Just ONE cookie with your milk?
Well sure, that sounds delightful.
But watch out if The Chunk's about
because he's also *spiteful*!

He'll grab those chocolate biscuits,
and he'll gobble EVERY one,
then when your mummy's back is turned,
he'll *really* have some fun . . .

He'll coat YOUR face with cookie crumbs,
and melted chocolate chips,
being sure to smudge the gooey,
gluey stuff around your lips.

Your mum will wag her finger,
and she'll meet you with a stare.
"You ate the LOT!" your mum
will shriek (how terribly unfair!).

And you'll protest: "I didn't, Mum!
It really wasn't me!"
The Chunk, while skipping out unseen,
will cackle with pure GLEE!

And off he'll go, the scallywag,
his wide eyes blazing wild,
looking for the next poor house
and unsuspecting child.

NEWS JUST IN:
It seems The Chunk has
ruined someone's wedding . . .

He slurped the chocolate fountain dry!
Now who knows WHERE he's heading!
LIVE!

So if YOU spot The Chunk,
please call this hotline right away.
He can't be left to swipe our chocs
like this for one more day.

Meanwhile, stay on
high alert – especially
while you snack.
'Cos be assured,
if he's not caught . . .

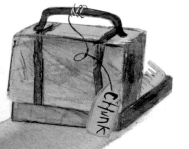